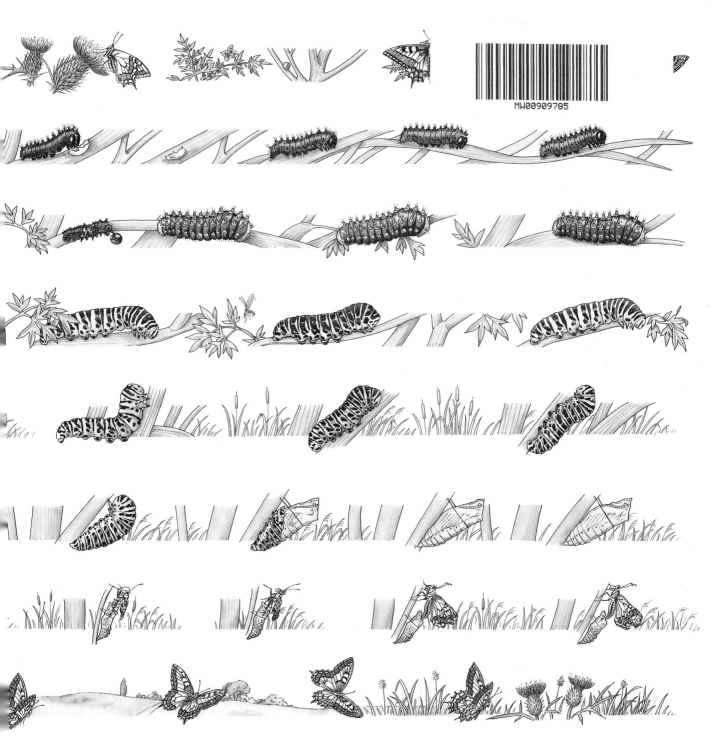

A DORLING KINDERSLEY BOOK

Written and Edited by Mary Ling
Art Editor Helen Senior
Production Louise Barratt
Illustrators Sandra Pond and Will Giles
Additional Photography Jane Burton
U.S. Editor B. Alison Weir
Special thanks to Worldwide Butterflies Ltd.

First American Edition, 1992
10 9 8 7 6 5 4 3

Published in the United States by
Dorling Kindersley Publishing, Inc., 95 Madison Avenue
New York, NY 10016

ISBN 1-56458-112-8
Library of Congress Catalog Card Number 92 - 52808

Color reproduction by J. Film Process Ltd, Singapore
Printed in Italy by L.E.G.O.

SEE HOW THEY GROW

BUTTERFLY

photographed by
KIM TAYLOR

DORLING KINDERSLEY, INC.
NEW YORK

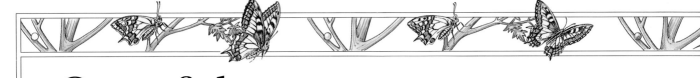

Out of the egg

I am a caterpillar. I grow inside my tiny yellow egg, which is no bigger than this dot —.

My mother is a butterfly. One day I will look like her.

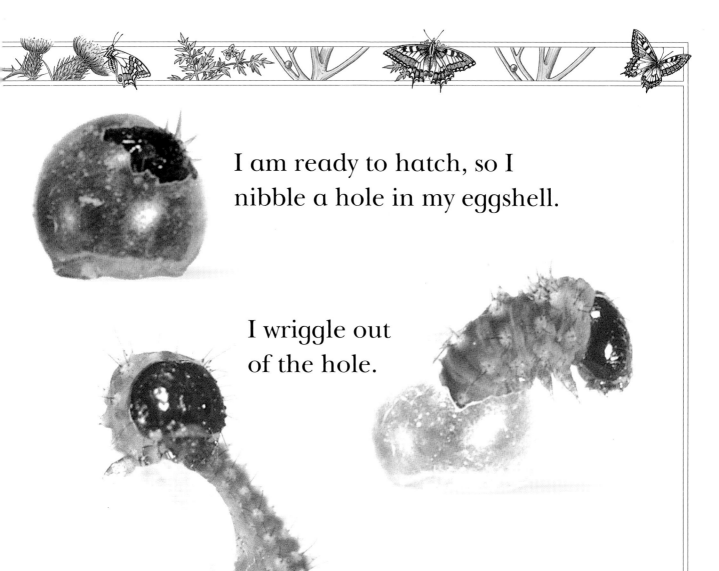

I am ready to hatch, so I nibble a hole in my eggshell.

I wriggle out of the hole.

At last I am free!

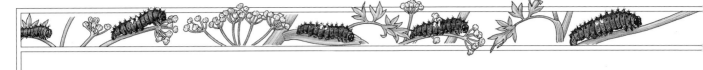

Growing bigger

I am one week old.
Each day I grow bigger.
I am always hungry.

My skin feels very
tight. I am starting
to shed my skin.

I wriggle out of my
old skin. My new skin
fits my plump body.

Soon I grow too
big for this skin.

Lots of legs

I am two weeks
old and my skin
is splitting again.

Now I have
bright stripes
on my body.

10

How many arms and legs do I have? I have six arms and ten legs.

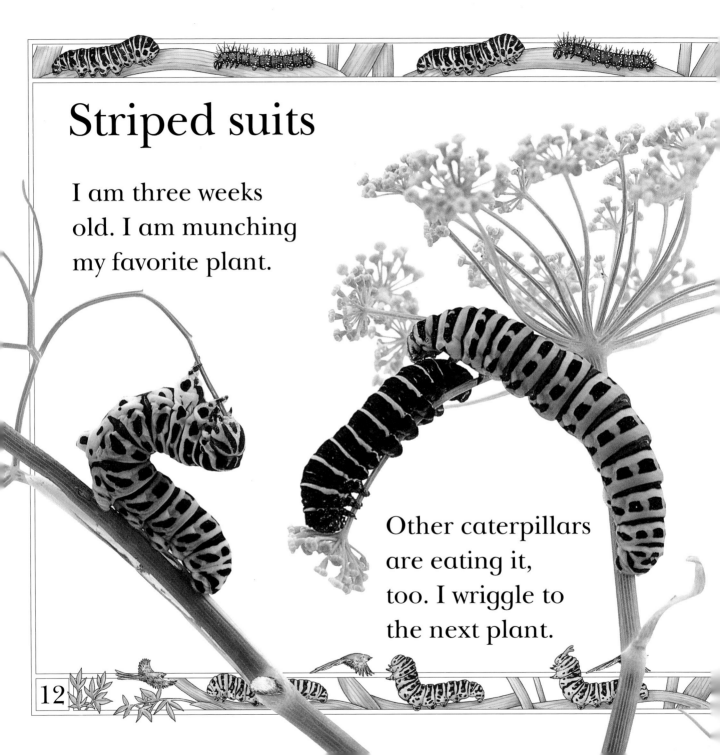

Striped suits

I am three weeks
old. I am munching
my favorite plant.

Other caterpillars
are eating it,
too. I wriggle to
the next plant.

While I am eating,
my striped suit
hides me from
danger.

I use my
orange horn
to scare
enemies away.

13

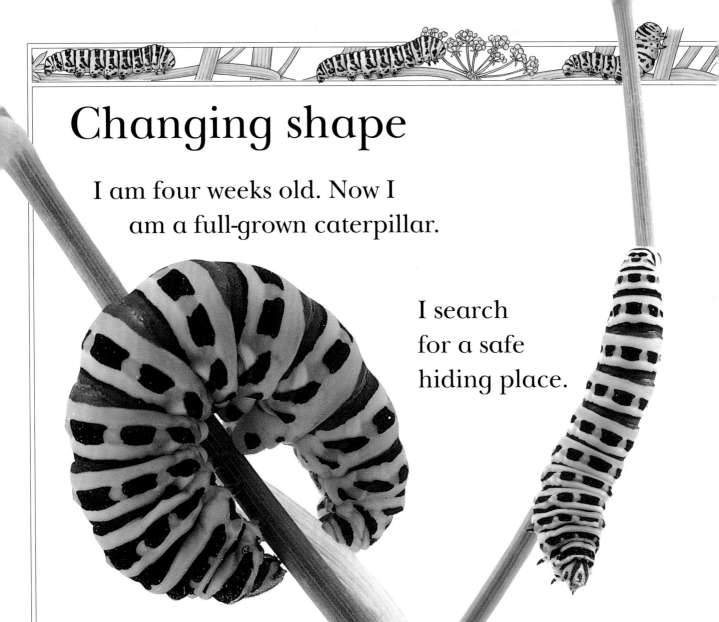

Changing shape

I am four weeks old. Now I
am a full-grown caterpillar.

I search
for a safe
hiding place.

My body is
changing shape.

I am not a caterpillar
anymore. I am
called a chrysalis.

15

Wings at last

When I am seven weeks old, I climb out of my pouch. I am a butterfly.

My new wings are crumpled and wet.

I rest for a while in the warm sunshine.

Soon my wings are flat. I can fly!

In the sunshine

Now I am eight weeks old and fully grown. My wings are strong. I can flutter through the meadow.

I drink sweet nectar from the flowers using my long tongue.

At last I look as colorful as my mother!

19

See how I grew

The egg   One week old   Two weeks old

Three weeks old   Four weeks old   Seven weeks old

Eight weeks old

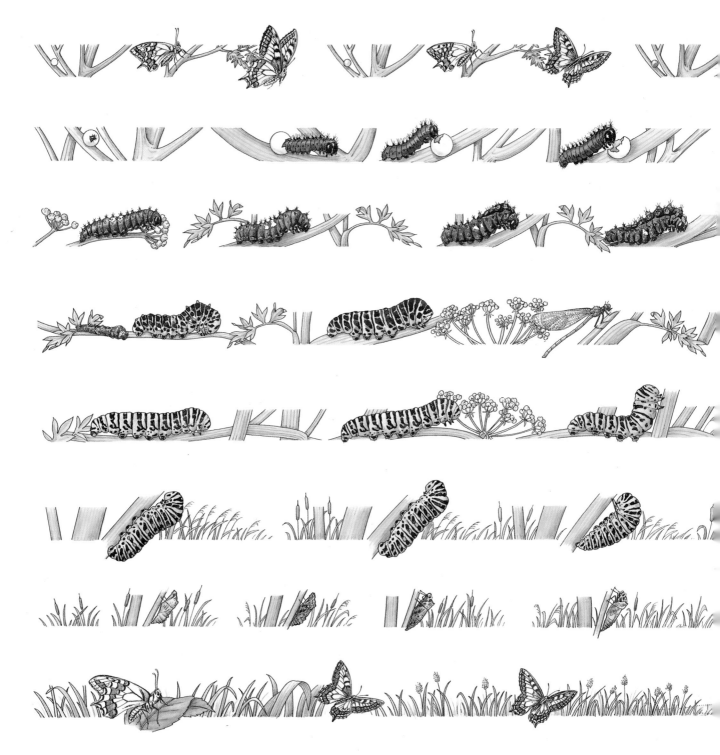